How Would Jesus Invest?

Breaking the
Poor Man's Mentality

Gayle M. Gilmore

xulon
PRESS

How Would Jesus Invest?
by Gayle M. Gilmore

Printed in the United States of America

Library of Congress Control Number: 2002117065
ISBN 1-591604-72-9

Xulon Press
11350 Random Hills Road
Suite 800
Fairfax, VA 22030
(703) 279-6511
XulonPress.com

To order additional copies, call 1-866-909-BOOK (2665).

DEDICATION

First, I give honor and glory to God and my Lord and Savior, Jesus Christ for keeping me in His care. I dedicate this book to the memory of my late parents, Elder Thomas Medley and Sister Annie Medley for "training me in the way that I should go, so that I would not depart from it."

I also dedicate this book to my dear husband, Rev. James E. Gilmore Sr. for being a true man and father to our children and my pillar of love and support for over 20 years. We are going to realize the "vision" together.

Candy and James Jr., you two are so precious to me. Being your mother has given me a glimpse of how God loves us all. In spite of what we do, He is still our Father.

ACKNOWLEDGEMENTS

A special thanks goes to my pastor, Rev. Warren E. Amlet and his lovely wife, Sister Irene Amlet for your consistent and prayerful support.

First Baptist Church South Portsmouth, you are indeed my family and love each and every one of you. You have encouraged, supported and challenged me to continuously grow in this faith. I will never forget you!

I would like to thank all my friends, near and far for your prayers for the success of this book.

Last, but not least, I pray for my enemies and those that don't know my Lord and Savior Jesus Christ....Yet!

I know that can change.

Introduction

"Before I formed thee in the belly I knew thee;
and before thou camest forth out of the
womb I sanctified thee, and I ordained
thee a prophet unto nations."
Jeremiah 1:5

You might be expecting one of those revealing stories where the author lets you in on a deep dark secret of their past. Sorry. I didn't grow up in a broken home. I haven't been physically or mentally abused. I haven't been without food or clothing or lights, or water, or shelter. I haven't been raped or molested. No, I didn't have an abortion or a baby out of wedlock and now regretting it. I am not a recovering drug addict or alcoholic who went through a 12 step program and discovered that when I put down one habit, I picked up another. I'm not a high school drop-out that later discovered I needed an education to make it. I haven't been to jail and spent time for some heinous crime. I haven't been diagnosed with some terminal disease. Sorry.

I praise God for His deliverance of people that have been healed and delivered of the circumstances that were mentioned previously. Their stories have been a source of inspiration for those that have had similar experiences. But that's not my story. My story appears to be very boring. Ordinary and average lives are not headlined on the front page of the newspaper and T.V. reports. You may occasionally find a "good deed highlight" in the smallest column of the daily news periodically. But for the most part, people want to hear the spectacular and bizarre.

But if the truth be told, there are thousands and thousands of people that have the same boring story that I have. We are not part of a "good ole boy" club, but this was planned for us from the beginning.

The prophet Jeremiah came to the realization that nothing just happens. Things are not just coincidental. God always has a plan. God revealed the plan to Jeremiah by stating that before Jeremiah even knew himself, before his very existence, He knew him. Not just his name, but what he was and even what his destiny would be. I know I'm right about the destiny part because God also tells Jeremiah , "For I know the thoughts that I think toward you, saith the Lord, thoughts of peace and not of evil, to give you an expected end." (Jeremiah 29:11)

Beginnings are so very important. Don't get me wrong. I know that many people have had horrible beginnings and the Lord brought them out. But why not plan good beginnings from the start. If you feel it's too late for you, (and really it's not too late), good beginnings can still start with your children or your grandchildren. The vicious cycle does not have to continue. God's plan for you is awesome.

I know it can be awesome. You see, I was adopted by loving parents when I was just a baby. God had me in his hand. Oftentimes, I think about the fact that I could have been born anywhere in the world. But God saw fit that I was born in America, a country whose roots are built on Godly principles. Have you ever imagined how it would be if you were born in a third-world country, a famine stricken country, a war torn country or an AIDS ravaged country?

We in America really don't know how blessed we are. The following poem expresses how God has lovingly guided my beginning to bring me to a meaningful end.

Loved, Not Adopted

She did not conceive me,
her body did not bare me,
But her love has shown me
All the things that I can be.

No blood of hers flows through my veins,
No D.N.A. to trace,
But to know that I belong
That fact, yet still remains.

From six days old she took me in
Not knowing where the trail might end.
An infant then, a girl of ten, a teen of constant change,
Now a lady being blessed to watch HER family blend.

She used no parent manual,
Except the Holy Book,
Its Golden rule and Beatitudes,

Formed what is called my ATTITUDE,

Now she's in her golden years,
White locks of wisdom fall round her ears,

Yet still she's there to calm my fears;
Was I adopted? Oh no, oh no:
Most definitely, I AM LOVED!

(Loved, Not Adopted, Gayle M. Gilmore,
Walk Through Paradise,
National Library of Poetry, 1995)

You see, you are not a stepchild in God's family. You are a joint-heir with Jesus Christ. You are entitled to an inheritance. That means that you are entitled TO HAVE IT ALL, both spiritually and financially.

You don't have to wait for someone to die to enjoy it. That was taken care of on the cross at Calvary over 2000 years ago. You can have it right now!

The question is how will you invest it? How would Jesus invest?

TABLE OF CONTENTS

Chapter 1

THAT BAD WORD...MONEY

A s we pay close attention to our nation's financial climate, especially the roller coaster ride of the stock market, we can't help from wondering what the future holds. Instead of "the Little Engine That Could," consistently climbing, chanting, "I think I can, I think I can, I think I can," the tune of the financial jingle is more like the lady on the T.V. commercial that says "I've fallen and I can't get up." Will the Enron, WorldCom and Martha Stewart scandals have a direct effect on our livelihood as we know it? How will world conditions such as terrorist attacks and rumors of war impact us?

As Christians, should we even care?

After all, the scriptures tell us "not to be anxious for nothing, to make our supplications known unto God." (Philippians 4:6). Although we should not become overly bent out of shape, this doesn't mean, however, that we just leave it up to chance. And what are these "supplications" or requests all about?

For the average Bible-toting, every-Sunday-going con-
gregant, the message is usually, "Hold on! Everything is
going to be alright. The Lord will provide." But the same
one-dollar bill that went in the offering basket in the small
wooden church 20 years ago is still tentatively being
dropped in the new cloth offering bags of the state-of-the-
art mega churches.

This book is not a put-down of how people give to
churches. It is also not another financial planning manual.
However, it can change our thinking and ability to give. It
could also whet your hunger for knowing how to handle
your resources in a more responsible way. There are many
good books out there. One I would highly recommend is
"God's Plan for Your Finances" by Dwight Nichols.

For a long time there has been a mindset that people,
especially saved, Christian folk, should not prosper. I'm not
just talking about prospering in the spirit either. I'm talking
about money. I'm talking about greenbacks. I'm not talking
about in the "sweet bye and bye." I'm talking about the
"nasty here and now." The lie from the pit of hell is that
"money is sinful." Satan has always had an art for twisting
the Word of God. And because of our lack of study of the
Word we take it "as is." The Bible states, "For the <u>love</u> of
money is the root of all evil: which while some coveted
after, they have erred from the faith and pierced themselves
through with many sorrows." (I Timothy 6:10) Well Gayle,
there it is. Money has made people lose the faith. I told you
money was bad.

Hold on there! The word "some" in that verse let's me
know that the majority has not been affected in this way.
This verse actually speaks about the "some" whose whole
entire focus is on money. So much so, that anything , legal
or illegal, will be performed to obtain it. Consequently, this
has not only caused "some" to lose faith but sometimes even
their physical lives.

Is it wrong to covet or have a strong desire for money? But I ask you, is it coveting, when daily needs are not met? Is it coveting when children are hungry and one can barely make it from paycheck to paycheck? I would not dare downplay the importance of storing spiritual riches. We are admonished to "labour not for the meat which perisheth but for the meat that endureth unto everlasting life, which the son of man shall give unto you: for him hath God the Father sealed." (John 6:27)

So where is the balance?

"Seek ye first the kingdom of God, and his righteousness and all these things shall be added unto you." (Matthew 6:33)

A Christian sister of mine asked " If God owns the cattle on a thousand hills, (Psalms 50:10), why can't I have just one sheep? Couldn't that possibly be one of the things that can be "added unto" me?

As we attempt to answer this question, "How would Jesus Invest?," we must get ready to accept sound investment advice from the Great Accountant himself. As a lot of you know, we started asking questions like "What would Jesus do?." I even saw a book on the shelf entitled, "What would Jesus eat?" If we are willing to follow Jesus' examples for everyday living and dieting, it would only make sense that we would follow his examples for managing and living abundantly with His resources!

"But my God shall supply all your need according to his riches in glory by Christ Jesus. (Philippians 4:19) Riches? Yes, riches by Jesus Christ. Spiritual AND earthly? Yes, spiritual AND earthly.

I looked up the word "rich" in the dictionary. It means "having goods, property and money in abundance." (Merriam-Webster) This should sound familiar. Jesus said ".... I am come that they may have life, and that they might have it more abundantly." (John 10:10) See, there's got to be earthly abundance for the Christian because we will not need anything when we get to heaven. (Revelation 22:1-5)

Chapter 2

"I Work Hard for the Money"

Donna Summers made that song famous back in the seventies. She added that since she worked so hard for it, "you better treat her right." When that alarm clock goes off in the morning, the thought of what Eve did in the garden has crossed our minds at least a few times. "Man, if only Eve hadn't eaten that fruit...I could turn back over for the rest of the day." But that is not altogether correct. Yes, it is true that because of the sin in the Garden of Eden, God cursed the ground and work became harder.

"...Cursed is the ground for thy sake; in sorrow shalt thou eat of it all the days of thy life. Thorns and thistles shall it bring forth to thee; and thou shalt eat the herb of the field. In the sweat of thy face shalt thou eat bread , till thou return unto the ground....." (Genesis 3:17-19)

No. Work did not start then. Adam had a job from the beginning. God gave man <u>dominion</u> over the fish of the sea and over the fowl of the air and over every living thing that moveth upon the earth" (Genesis 1:28) Having dominion doesn't just mean looking at it.

"And the Lord God took the man and put him into the garden of Eden to dress it and to keep it." Genesis 2:15

Although naming animals (Genesis 2:20) and having natural sprinklers (Genesis 2:6) was not a back breaking task, God never meant for man to be idle.

God nor Jesus dealt with lazy people. God called Noah to build an ark, (even before Noah knew what an ark was!). Abraham was a world traveler. Moses planned and took care of sheep. David also tended sheep and killed giants. Ruth gathered sheaves. Lydia sold purple cloth. Jesus' disciples were fishermen, tax collectors, tentmakers etc. Paul a.k.a. Saul went from persecuting Christians to tormenting the devil. So, I don't know how some of us believe we should live on flowery beds of ease.

Jesus learned the trade of carpentry from his earthly father, Joseph. Jesus' ministry was even a physical one. He was constantly on the move. He was trekking through the wilderness, hopping on ships, preaching on mountains and turning tables over in the temple.

God even worked.

"When I consider thy heavens, the <u>work</u> of thy fingers, the moon and the stars, which thou hast ordained (set in place)" Psalm 8:3.

So you think it's unfair that we have to work to enjoy a bowl of cornflakes. If you think that's something, God even instructed us to take lessons from an ant.

"Go to the ant, thou sluggard; consider her ways and be wise: Which having no guide, overseer or ruler, provideth her meat in the summer and gathereth her food in the harvest" Proverbs 6:6-8

When you don't work, you shouldn't eat. (II Thessalonians 3:10) Not even a bowl of Tony the Tiger flakes. No matter how Greeeaaaaat! they are.

Chapter 3

It's God's Way or the Poor Way

Part I

Before long, you will figure out that I like to relate to songs. I started out the first chapter with a secular song and I'm going to do the same here. Frank Sinatra, "Old Blue Eyes" used to sing "My Way." It tells the story about someone that has gone through a lot of experiences in their life. But instead of giving up or failing, one rises above it all and declares that the victory is won because "I did it my way."

Well, that could have been my song, before I was saved. I wouldn't be up typing this chapter at 3 a.m. in the morning if it was "my way." I don't usually get up this time of the morning but last night God had put such an urgency on my heart. In talking with God, I told Him, "If you really want me to write this, wake me up at 3 a.m., without the alarm clock (I didn't want to disturb my husband since he gets up at 4:45 a.m. for work)." "My way" would be to turn over, not wake up, and do several rounds of hitting the snooze button three times after 6 a.m. Since I became "a new creature in Christ, old things (ways) have passed away, and behold (look at this), all things (ways) are new." As a matter of fact, "my way" ultimately leads to destruction.

There's a way that seemeth right unto a man, but the end thereof are the ways of death. Proverbs 14:12

The issue is obedience to God. This effects every aspect of our life. And although we're talking about both spiritual and financial investment, obedience to God balances it all out.

"For ye have the poor always with you...." Matthew 26:11

We read this, and for the most part we think, it's just how things are always going to be. It just sounds hopeless. If we look at the context or setting of this verse, we see that Jesus said this in response to those disciples and spectators that criticized a woman for pouring the precious ointment from the alabaster box. The critics said that this sweet perfume could have been sold for a lot of money and given to the poor. Even if the disciples' motives were pure, Jesus would have still stood up for the woman because of her obedience to the spirit of ministering unto him. Verse 11 concludes with the fact "...but me ye have not always." Therefore, Jesus said leave her alone.

"......for she has wrought a good work upon me. (v. 10b)

"For in that she hath poured this ointment on my body, she did it for my burial. Verily I say unto you, Wheresoever

this gospel shall be preached in the whole world, there shall also that this, that this woman hath done, be told for a memorial of her." (v. 12-13)

Because of her obedience, this unnamed woman is still honored today. Many messages have been preached. Gospel great, Ce Ce Winans, even wrote the song, Alabaster Box, that has become a hit. We're talking about obedience.

Does this mean that Jesus didn't care for the poor? Certainly not! There are many scriptures that support the fact that Jesus was very much concerned for the poor. He was so concerned that not only did He look at the situation and said, "What a shame. What a pity," but he moved with compassion (love in action) and supplied their need. From providing thousands of fish sandwiches to healing people exactly where they hurt, Jesus was on it.

Have you ever asked the question, Why are their poor people anyway? Did God intend for us to have less than what He can give? Glad you asked! We've got to go back to the Garden of Eden.

Adam and Eve were rich in the sense that they had it all; Food, land, companionship, employment, beautiful surroundings, good weather and most of all the presence and love of a heavenly Father. Watch this though. I had to be careful not to say clothing because that was not a need initially.

Oops! There it is!

There was no need of clothing until the sin. What was the sin? Eating the fruit in itself was not the issue. It was the fact that eating the fruit from the very tree that God told them not to eat from was a blatant act of disobedience. Get this.

We become poor, when as a result of disobedience to God, an additional need is created.

Now, after the fall, clothes became an issue. Man needed an additional covering besides his skin to protect him and cover his shame. Just think about the money that would be saved if we didn't have wardrobe expenses.

Allow me to spend some time on this concept of obedience. As we examine today's society we know that disobedience to God is rampant. For example, we allow all types of poisonous chemicals in our bodies through cigarettes, drugs and alcohol when God tells us in His word that our bodies are temples. (I Corinthians 3:16-17) This oftentimes, creates the need for money to support the habit, unnecessary health expenses, not to mention a less than satisfying quality of life. We commit fornication and adultery, which is a direct violation to God's commandments (Exodus 20:14) Then we are perplexed when our homes break up and the income diminishes and generational curses begin to breed. Disobedient children do not heed the instruction of parents (Exodus 20:12) and being unprepared for life, live less than and sometimes cut their abundant life short in the process. And the list goes on.

The Bible bears out the fact, over and over the many episodes of Israel's soap opera cycle:

Disobedience, Punishment, Forgiveness, Obedience, Restoration
Disobedience, Punishment, Forgiveness, Obedience, Restoration
Disobedience, Punishment, Forgiveness, Obedience, Restoration

The punishment or discipline stage gradually eats away at our resources of joy, peace and prosperity each time. For example, when Israel disobeyed, God caused a famine or allowed Israel's enemies to overtake them. Israel would ask for forgiveness and start being obedient again. Restoration would occur. But although the rains came and armies were defeated, they ended up with less than what they began with.

Chapter 4

COMMERCIAL BREAK

I've got to stop right here for a commercial break. Today is September 17, 2002.

I've already been up since 3 a.m. writing on the computer on this book. Yesterday evening, two things happened. My husband and I were watching a sermon by Bishop T.D. Jakes from a series of sermons entitled, "What You Don't Know, Can Hurt You." In one part of the sermon he was talking about what God had told Joshua. In Joshua 1:3, God told Joshua, "Every place that the sole of your foot shall tread upon, that have I given unto you, as I said unto Moses." Bishop Jakes went on to demonstrate by taking big steps across the stage, this promise. Bishop Jakes went on to say that "if you can walk on it, you can put your hand on it." Also, I was reading a book entitled "Praying the Scriptures: Communicating With God in His Own Words," by Judson Cornwall. In this book, the author emphasizes the importance of the scripture in our prayers. One passage reads, "What the Holy Spirit quickens us to see in the Scriptures is the <u>will</u> of God. We should pray it (the scriptures); proclaim it; practice it. It will put faith and fire into our prayers. As a matter of fact, it is often something seen or remembered in the Scriptures that initiates our praying in the first place."

God has been leading my husband and I towards a vision that will meet the needs of a dying world. We have been serving, teaching, and preaching for a number of years and will continue to do so. We have been placed in strategic areas at our jobs, in our church and throughout the community to serve. But the vision is bigger. I don't know how God is going to do it. It's none of my business, but I know God is going to work in a supernatural way to bring it to past. We don't have to wait until the battle is over. We're going to shout right now!

Chapter 5

It's God's Way
or the Poor Way

Part II

I would like to know who came up with the theological concepts of "perfect" and "permissive " wills of God? It goes without saying that God is perfect in everything. Why would He be permissive about it? It's like a parent telling a child not to touch a hot stove. The will or command of the parent is right and will prevent the child from getting hurt. If the child touches it anyway and cries "OUCH," did the parent "permit" it? No, of course not. The child made a choice on his own and did it his way and was burnt. The only reason why we haven't been struck by a bolt of lightning or turned into a pillar of salt is not because of permissiveness but because of His grace and mercy.

Many people believe that the turning point in Jesus' life was the miracles, the crucifixion or the resurrection. But I think the moment in history that determined our fate happened in the garden of Gethsemane. Being God in the flesh, Jesus did not want to face the agony of crucifixion. Consider the story in Mark's rendering.

"Abba, Father, all things are possible unto thee; take away this cup from me : <u>nevertheless</u> not what I will, but what thy wilt." Mark 14:36

It was clear that this was an agonizing moment. Luke's gospel describes that this moment was so traumatic that as he prayed under such intense pressure, "his sweat was as it were drops of blood falling down to the ground." (Luke 22:44) His pores pushed out blood as well as sweat. Everything hung in the balance. Jesus knew that the Father could have made this easier. As a matter of fact, God could have just spoken it and the debt would have been paid. Jesus knew the power of God. Jesus could have died in his sleep. He could have been translated (caught up from the earth into heaven) like Enoch.(Genesis 5:24)

"By faith Enoch was translated that he should not see death; and was not found, because God had translated him: for before his translation he had this testimony, that he pleased God." Hebrews 11:5

Without a shadow of a doubt, Jesus pleased God. Couldn't he had died a more dignified death or how about no death at all? He could beat up Satan and be done with it. But, NEVERTHELESS! Jesus made it clear that regardless of the outcome, "not what I will" (not my will to be or strong desire) but "what thy wilt" (Your will for me or strong desire). If human will had taken control, the outcome would have been different. There is no gray area regarding will. It's God's will versus our will.

"The steps of a good man are ordered by the Lord: and he (the Lord) delighteth in his way." Psalms 37:23

Granted, Jesus' upcoming appointment with a cross was not "delightful." But to act in any way contrary to the will of God would have been rebellion. Rebellion is sin. What we fail to realize is that since God has our best interest in mind and can see further ahead than we could ever see, even in the direst of situation, God knows the glorious end.

"But [Jesus] made himself of no reputation and took upon him the form of a servant and was made in the likeness of men: And being found in fashion as a man, he humbled himself and became obedient unto death, even the death of the cross. Wherefore God hath highly exalted him and given him a name which is above every name." Philippians 2:7-9

Look at what Jesus would have missed out on (life, exaltation, honorable name...) if it happened any other way.

There is an underlying will imbedded in our will. It is the diabolical plan of Satan to woo us into a false & temporary sense of security. The plot thickens as inattention to God's will ultimately leads to rebellion.

"Again, the devil taketh him [Jesus] into an exceeding high mountain, and showeth him all the kingdoms of the world and the glory of them; and saith unto him All these things will I give thee, if thou wilt fall down and worship me." Matthew 4:8-9

How in the world could the devil give Jesus something that the devil didn't possess in the first place? That's like writing a check, knowing that you don't have two nickels to rub together. The legal name for this crime is called uttering which is closely related to forgery. Uttering is committed when "any person who utters (speaks) and employs as true a forged writing or instrument knowing at the time it to be forged with intent to defraud another person to the prejudice of another person's legal rights." For example, the news reported that a lady fraudently made or forged a check 'from an insurance company' and used the check to buy a car. She knew that money wasn't hers. She spoke and acted as though it was hers. People go to jail for that. Satan "utters" to our spirit and shows us things he already knows is a lie as he parades delusions of grandeur that lead to lust that ultimately lead to destruction.

"For all that is in the world, the lust of the flesh and the lust of the eyes and the pride of life,.." I John 2:16

The devil tried to make Jesus think that the only way that He could be rich would be through evil means. That's why playing the lottery, gambling, dealing drugs, get rich schemes, prostitution, etc. do not work. The "live for the moment" facade acts as blinders or sunshades to block the consequences. Satan conveniently leaves some details out. He doesn't happen to mention that gambling & playing lotto leads to addiction and further loss of money. Going to jail and getting hooked on drugs is never taken seriously or communicated effectively by the dark prince. Any inkling of a sexually transmitted disease, AIDS, unwanted pregnancy and violence associated with prostitution is reduced to sweet nothings whispered by the Hades pimp.

What did Jesus do? He squared off with Satan using the Word of God, which is the sword of the Spirit. (Ephesians 5:17) See, Satan is trying to have the upper hand. We cannot be polite and cordial to him. We can't plead with him. "Oh

Devil, will you please leave me alone? St-o-p!" We can't be whimpering like a scared little child on the playground facing a bully. Jesus commanded with authority.

"Get thee thence, Satan: for it is written, Thou shalt worship the Lord thy God, and him only shalt thy serve." Matthew 4:10

Worship depicts recognizing who God is. Among the many names that describe the character of God is Jehovah-jireh meaning God, My Provider. Knowing and believing this from a personal standpoint opens the door to bountiful provision. But just opening a door and peeking through it, does not let that long-time friend in or gives the stranger refuge from the storm. Obedience is the icing on the cake that completes the order that the Divine Baker desires for us to enjoy.

If we think about Abraham, we see this picture clearly. Abraham was instructed to take his promised son, Isaac, to a mountain and use him as a sacrifice. Isaac did not know what was really going to happen. But he became curious when he noticed that Abraham had two of the three ingredients that were needed for the sacrifice. There was the knife. There was the fire. Where was the sacrifice? Abraham told his son that God would provide for Himself a sacrifice. The fact that Abraham merely knew this was not enough. He had to act on it. And Abraham did! Abraham was right to the point of bringing down the knife to stab Isaac. God knew at that point that He could trust Abraham in the provision that was about to be given. Abraham proved he would be obedient to the will of God, no matter what.

Today, most of us are not called to such severe tests as Abraham's. One reason may be that we tend to disobey even the smallest requests. Sometimes when the preacher asks a congregation to merely give God a hand clap of praise or a "yes" to the truths of the Word, some don't do it. It's as if you had asked them to go to the cross and be crucified. Hebrews 13:15 says that "by him therefore let us offer the sacrifice of praise to God continually, that is the fruit of our lips giving thanks to his name." When we sacrifice something, we give something that we necessarily don't care to give but we give or do it any way.

There is a sweet return for the investment of obedience. A father is more inclined to give and support an obedient son. When this happens, whatever is the father's can also be the son's. That includes influence and power of the Heavenly Father transferred to the Son. We must understand that God is using that vessel of clay as a messenger to bring you closer to heir-ship with His Son through the call of simple submission to His will. When we do this, this gives us the right to have it all.

I learned this at an early age.

The only thing that I didn't like about Christmas, Easter, Mother's Day and Father's Day was the fact that I had to memorize a recitation. This was the ritual where Mama would select a passage or poem that I would have to memorize and recite at church programs for these occasions. She demanded that it would be spoken loudly and clearly while standing straight with hands down to my side without fidgeting. I didn't like it but I did it. I dared not to do it right. She believed in the adage, "Whether the task be great or small, do it well or none at all." Little did I know at the time that this was preparing me in combination with the call of the Holy Ghost to be able to stand in front of audiences to proclaim His Word.

Another thing that Mama would do was to make me showcase my ability to play the flute. I would dread when company came to the house. Even when I was just beginning to learn to play, after a while, she would proudly share, "You know Gayle is playing the flute. Gayle, get your flute out and play for Miss So and So." Again, I did it; sometimes begrudgingly and hesitantly. But again little did I know, that Mama was preparing me to step out, fight fear and cultivate my skills that ultimately lead me to earn my bachelor's degree in music education that lead to me earning a master's degree in guidance counseling. Incidentally, I still play the flute for my students as a guidance director.

"Blessed is everyone that feareth the Lord; that walketh in his ways. For thou shalt eat the labour of thine hands: happy shalt thou be and it shall be well with thee." Psalms 128:1-2

Mama had a reverent fear of God, and was determined to "train me in the way I should go." This, in turn, instilled within me both a trembling and reverent fear of Mama and God! Now I am now able to enjoy and eat the fruits of my labor. It is well with me. Thank you, Mama.

"But thou shalt remember the Lord thy God: for it is he that giveth thee power to get wealth, that he may establish his covenant which he sware unto thy father, as it is this day." Deuteronomy 8:18

What is this "power" that is mentioned here? It is simply referring to the human means by which you can obtain wealth. Is it your job? Is it your education? Is it your talents and abilities? Not really. There are employed people that are poor. There are educated people with PhD's that are living under bridges. There are talented people in jail. What is it then?

Here's something that's going to blow your mind. Deuteronomy 28: 1-14 lists all of these awesome blessings that we are promised. Did you hear me? I said PROMISED to us if we will just obey Him. God doesn't break His promises. Look at this!

"If you fully obey the Lord your God by keeping all the commands I am giving you today, the Lord your God will exalt you above all the nations of the world.

You will experience all these blessings if you obey the Lord your God:

You will be blessed in your towns and in the country.

You will be blessed with many children and productive fields.

You will be blessed with fertile herds and flocks.

You will be blessed with baskets overflowing with fruit, and with kneading bowls filled with bread.

You will be blessed wherever you go, both in coming and in going.

The Lord will conquer your enemies when they attack you. They will attack you from one direction, but they will scatter from you in seven!

The Lord will bless everything you do and fill your storehouses with grain.

The Lord your God will bless you in the land he is giving you.

If you obey the commands of the Lord your God and walk in his ways, the Lord will establish you as his holy people as he solemnly promised to do. Then all the nations will see that you are a people claimed by the Lord, and they will stand in awe of you.

The Lord will give you an abundance of good things in the land he swore to give your ancestors—many children, numerous livestock, and abundant crops.

The Lord will send rain at the proper time from his rich treasury in the heavens to bless all the work you do.

You will lend to many nations, but you will never need to borrow from them.

If you listen to these commands of the Lord your God and carefully obey them, the Lord will make you the head and not the tail, and you will always have the upper hand.

You must not turn away from any of the commands I am giving you today to follow after other gods and worship them.
(New Living Translation)

WOW! Why do most pastors keep silent on these scriptures? It could be the fear that they feel that their parishioners would put more emphasis on materialistic gain rather than the spiritual riches of God. The rest of Deuteronomy 28, beginning at verse 15 gives us the flip side of disobeying God. We see the curses of disobedience. I believe that if ministers are truly anointed and rooted in the Word of God, they would be unctioned to feed their flock balanced portions. They would not starve the sheep nor make them gluttons. The message would be that if "God gives us the power to get wealth," this also means that this same God can keep us in check and keep us balanced.

Again, *"The steps of a good man are* [still] *ordered by the Lord."*—rich or poor.

Chapter 6

IF JESUS WAS POOR, WHY DID HE HAVE A TREASURER?

Could you imagine Bill Gates, one of the richest men in the world, not utilizing the services of a banker or an accountant? Since God created everything and Jesus is the King of Kings and Lord of Lords, wouldn't it make sense that he might need a treasurer, even it was merely to witness that he can indeed " supply all our need according to his riches in heaven?" (Philippians 4:19) I can also imagine that even if Jesus had not come to earth in the flesh, there would still be some financially astute angels, thoroughly checking accounts of withdrawals and disbursements as authorized by the chief CEO—God.

"The foxes have holes and the birds of the air have nests; but the Son of man hath not where to lay his head."
Matthew 8:20

Many preachers use this verse to make church folks think that Jesus was non-chalant about money. They would have you believe that He was so down and out, that he couldn't even afford a place to sleep. This whole mentality would be an insult to many of the patriarchs in the Old Testament. Why in the world would David declare, "I have been young, and now am old; yet have I not seen the <u>righteous</u> forsaken nor his seed begging bread.?" Psalm 37: 25. Who's more righteous than the Christ?

However, as we look at the full context, we find that a scribe had just announced that he would follow Jesus wherever He went. Jesus wanted the scribe to realize that this was going to be an on-the-go journey. He didn't want the scribe to think this was going to be a 9 to 5 workday. He did not want there to be any confusion concerning the fact that this scribe would not be able to come home every night and stretch out on his Quilt-A- Pedic or Sealy mattress. There was no way of telling where they would end up at the close of any given day.

Think about it. Even though the Bible is silent between the time that Jesus was twelve years old and the start of his public ministry at around age twenty-nine or thirty, it would be safe to say that Jesus had to be gainfully employed doing something. We know that his parents were responsible towards their financial circumstances. This is evident because of the very purpose that Joseph went to Bethlehem in the beginning—- to be taxed while Jesus was in the womb of Mary. Jesus could have sustained himself by working as a carpenter, the trade that his earthly father, Joseph, had taught him. We could probably go as far to say that since he was the oldest child of Mary, he helped the family, both financially and spiritually, especially after Joseph died. For Jesus to speak about money, stewardship and accountability to such a large extent in the New Testament lets us know this was an important issue to Him.

Among the many references that Jesus uses, we see how he uses a lot of farming terms, especially as it pertains to the law of sowing and reaping. Crops and harvest were used in Biblical times in the same way that we use money today. The most significant rule is that you reap <u>more</u> than you sow—good or bad. The result is always multiplied. For example, if you plant a few kernels of corn, you are not going to get back the exact number. Why even plant them in the first place, if that's the case? Instead, there will be many ears of corn with hundreds upon hundreds of kernels on each ear. If we sow good seed, the return will be bountiful and running order. And in the same way, if we sow bad seed, we will multiply our sorrows.

It is important to note that not only did Jesus select men that readily followed him, but he selected men that had previously worked. Some were fishermen that survived off the bounty of the seas. There was a tax collector who understood accounting. There's a few that we don't know what they were employed as before but knowing Jesus' attitude about work ethics, they did something. Then there was Judas.

Money necessitates the need for a treasurer. Not only did Judas "hold the money bag," but he also helped himself from it. We know this because he did not consult with any of the other disciples when he decided to pay Jesus' enemies thirty pieces of silver. (maybe he thought it would be a silent, sound investment with many returns.)

But even with Judas' kleptomaniac tendencies, there was always enough money to take care of obligations and even some luxuries. Don't forget that there was a cost to rent out the Upper Room for the Last Supper. You know you can't have a banquet at the Hilton Hotel without paying. The hall was laid out and fully furnished. It was even considered that when Jesus told Judas to "go and do whatever he would do and do it quickly" that Jesus was telling Judas to take care of the bill for this gathering. However, we know that this was the farthest from Judas' mind.

When it came to paying taxes, he was not a Boston Tea party sympathizer, using the excuse of "taxation without representation.

"Render therefore unto Caesar (the government) the things which are Caesar's; and unto God the things that are God's." Matthew 22:21

He demonstrated this on another occasion when some folks asked Peter did his master (Jesus) pay the temple tax. Peter replied, "Of course he does." And before Peter could say anything else, Jesus challenged Peter with a question. Jesus asked Peter which people did he think that the kings taxed. Home people or foreigners? Peter said foreigners. Jesus said, "Well then, the citizens are free. But to avoid offending anyone, go and hook the first fish you catch from the sea, open its mouth, take the money out and pay the tax for me and you." Jesus didn't let his "good be evil spoken of." He was accountable even when He didn't necessarily have to be.

What was Jesus' job title? Jesus started his line of work at 12 years old. It was not called child exploitation in his case. We discover what it is when Jesus and His earthly parents, Mary and Joseph traveled to Jerusalem for the feast. Families came in caravans. Evidently, it was thought with he was at another part of the entourage and didn't realize he was missing until it was time to go home. Frantically, they searched for him and finally find him in the temple, talking and asking questions Mary, responding as any scared mother in this situation would react, asked him why had he scared them half to death. He makes his big announcement.

"But why did you need to search? he asked. You should have known that I would be in my Father's house. (or about my Father's business) Luke 2:49

I would like to give him the title of "executor" of His Father's estate. In today's terms, this is a person who carries out the wishes for someone who is deceased or who can no longer speak for themselves.

That is exactly what our job title should be as well. We should execute the tasks that God would have us to do. The best way to do this is to keep his commandments.

As a sidebar, Mary really kept her cool by "pondering these things in her heart." As a mother myself, I'm not sure if I could have just settled it like that. I think this would be where I would have to apply the scripture concerning "sparing the rod and spoiling the child."

This episode in Jesus' life also illustrates early preparation. Ask any successful businessman. Jesus did not just start being equipped spiritually at the last 3 years of his ministry and life. Besides the spiritual aspect, I can't help from believing that some monetary banking was in place.

"For which of you, intending to build a tower, sitteth not down first and counteth the cost whether he have sufficient to finish it?" Luke 14:28

Even Jesus did not walk into circumstances blindly. In this context, Jesus had just finished talking about taking up one's cross and following Him. Why would Jesus suggest that we do something that He would not do himself? He desires that we be prepared on all fronts. Imagine going on a trip without considering the distance, the costs, checking out our transportation, etc.

Chapter 7

SOMETIMES IT JUST DOESN'T MAKE SENSE

(Faith)

Sometimes Jesus asks us to do things that seem ridiculous or insignificant. We may wonder how in the world does it fit into the overall plan that God has for our lives. There are many instances in the Bible where men and women of God were called upon to do things that would make you think God was crazy!

"Abraham, kill your son. I know that you shouldn't kill. (I'm going to let my friend, Moses, record that later.) But take this son that I promised you and do what I say. I know you really love this boy. I know I'm right because when I told you and your wife about this boy, you tried to hurry the process by trying to help me out and having Ishmael. I love

Ishmael, too. But that wasn't the one. I guess you think I'm suffering from some type of Alzheimer's disease. I know it doesn't make sense. I told you that you would have so many generations of children that they would outnumber the grains of sand. But I need you to take him to Moriah and kill him. Even Isaac is even going to wonder what you're doing. I'll take care of him though."

"Noah, build an ark. You don't know what an ark is? That's Ok. I'll give you information for the materials you need and the measurements and everything. I need you to build this because it's going to rain for a long time. I know you see the sunshine now. But it's going to rain buckets later on. And by the way, I know you are not a zookeeper, but I need you to round up two of every animal.

One male and one female. I will give you the wisdom to tell the difference. It's going to seem silly, but that's OK."

"Moses, take off your shoes. This is holy ground. You see me in this bush that's burning but you don't see it breaking down into ashes. You're going to be used by me, but you won't be broken down. I'll be with you. You will only need a rod. You are going to tell the Pharaoh to free my people who are in bondage. You may not be able speak too clear, but I'll speak for you. I'm going to tell you to part seas and speak to rocks that will bring forth water. It sounds silly but it's going to be OK. You're going to be my friend. You're going to be such a close friend, I'm going to write commandments on stone with my finger. I trust you to share this with my people for generations."

"Joshua, Moses, my servant is dead. You are next in line. I will be with you like I was with Moses. I've got a battle I want you to lead. It's against that walled up city of Jericho. The only weapons you will need are trumpets and a shout

from the people. But I don't want you to do this right away. There's going to be a warm-up exercise for six days. Just have everyone just march around the wall for six days very quietly. The final performance will be on the seventh day. It's going to look silly. But that's OK."

"David, defeat the giant with a slingshot. I know that in comparison with Goliath, you look like L'il Bow Wow going up against Mike Tyson. It looks like a no-brainer. I know you haven't had any military training. I don't even want you to try on any armor. None of it would fit anyway. But just look at it the same way you did when you protected your sheep by killing the bear and the lion. This time you're looking out for My sheep."

"Naaman, go take a bath. I know you don't think that taking a simple bath will rid you of this dreadful disease that they call leprosy. It's bad enough that people don't even want to be around you. But to add insult to injury, you paid my prophet to help you get rid of this stuff and he had the unmitigated gall to not even greet you. He just sent you to go to a river and dip. Not even a clean river. He wants you to go to that filthy Jordan river. I know the river is dirty and one dip would be enough but you need to dip seven times. You might think it's silly and rude. But wouldn't it be something if it really worked?"

"Joseph, marry Mary. I know she's pregnant with a child that's not even yours. You must think Mary takes you for a fool .No one has ever heard about a woman conceiving a child with out sexual intercourse. I know you're worried about what the fellas are going to think. But it's alright. I have a special plan for this child. I assure you that everything is on the up and up.

"Mary, get someone to roll the stone from your brother's, Lazarus, tomb. Yes, he's been dead for a few days. He's a little green around the gills. I know it doesn't seem right that I'm telling you to do this. After all, I could have come before he died. You ministered and served me in Bethany when I passed through on my way to Jerusalem. You and your sister Martha were always close friends. It hurt me to hear the news. But I want to show what friends are for."

"Blind man, let me put some spit on your eyes. I'm going to mix it with dirt. I know it doesn't seem sanitary. After I apply this, you can go down and wash it all out. What's that blind man? Did you say that you could see, but from what you've felt and experienced, the people don't look quite right? Did you say they look like trees? Let me remedy that. What do you see now, blind man? Did you say you could see clearly now, not because the rain is gone, but because the Doctor was in the house?"

"Peter, let me borrow your boat. I know you are a fisherman but I'm doing another type of fishing. I just need you to let me use it to go a ways in the water and talk to my people. After that, you can go fishing. I know you are the expert, but I need you to fish a different way. I know it sounds strange, since you have already fished earlier and didn't even get a bite. Just watch and see what happens.

"Gayle, preach my word. I know you think you were not ready but I've known you for a long time. It didn't make sense to you. I knew you before you were even thought of in the womb. I know I called your husband first. And that is how I do things; in order. But I called you, my daughter. So you are a female. So what? I am no respecter of persons. I've got a mission for you. You have seen and experienced how I have done some unbelievable things in your life and

I'm not finished. Remember, how I took you in the beginning and placed you in the care of God fearing parents. Remember, how I protected and gave you wisdom through-out your early school days .I know you won't forget how I spared your life until you got saved on that college campus and truly became my very own. Look at how I have blessed you with good health. Look at how I have moved you from one success to another. Look at the talents I have given you. Look at the beautiful children I've given you. Remember how I restored breathing to your 3 month old son after you and your husband so graciously dedicated him to Me. Remember how I placed angels around your daughter and son in the car accident. The car was totaled but I was more interested in those precious ones because I've got stuff for them to do, too. You go girl!"

"Jesus, go to the cross and be crucified. You are my only begotten Son. Because I love them so much, you're the only one that can carry this out. Son, although I realize you have not done anything wrong, it has to be this way. It doesn't seem fair, Son. I know I sent you down to earth against your wishes. I made you wear the clothes of filthy flesh. I know. I heard you praying in agony in the garden and I know how you feel. You are getting ready to be the scapegoat for so many. Not only will you be the sacrifice for the crowd around you but even for those who have not even been born yet. I know you wanted this to happen in a different way. You are such an obedient boy and I will not forget you. I may have to turn my back on you briefly because of my nature. But don't forget I love you. You will always be my beloved one. One in who I am well pleased."

Yes, sometimes it just doesn't make sense.

There are four things that we must keep in mind when Jesus calls us to do the seemingly doesn't-make-sense, you-mean-me, are-you-sure types of things.

Number one.

God always has a plan.

He is always devising a way for us to bring glory to his name. Through his meticulous thoughts, the map is already laid out to guide us from the beginning to the end. God knew the plan for Jesus even from the Garden of Eden. Here's what God let Satan in on from the beginning.

"And I will put enmity between thee and the woman ,and between thy seed and her seed.(Mary's seed who is Jesus.) It shall bruise thy head(Jesus is going to defeat Satan) and thou shalt bruise his heel(Satan, you are only going to be a mild nuisance to Jesus). Genesis 3:15

God's plan for our salvation was not an after thought. He knew all the time.

God's plan for your life was not an after thought either. Notice Jeremiah's declaration.

"Before I formed thee in the belly I knew thee; and before thou camest forth out of the womb I sanctified thee, and I ordained thee a prophet unto the nations." Jeremiah 1:5

"For I know the thoughts I think toward you, saith the Lord, thoughts of peace, and not of evil, to give you an expected end." Jeremiah 29:11

Just like Jeremiah, God knew you before you knew yourself. God has the whole blueprint laid out. Like an architect, he has accurately calculated all the measurements and specifications. But what happens sometimes, we don't want to follow the blueprint. Instead, of coming to the "expected end," we end up with a flawed product. In many instances, we have to go back and follow the directions to the letter.

Number two.

He knows what He is doing.

When Moses was told by God that he was to lead the people out of Egypt, Moses had a lot of questions. Sometimes, people think it's wrong to question God in certain matters. According to God, just like some of my old teachers used to tell me, "There is never a stupid question." God wants us to know Him and who better to enquire in than the One who commissions us. It is God's choice on how He will answer. Therefore when Moses asked, "What shall I say when I tell the people that the God of their fathers has sent me and they ask me what your name is?" God said "I AM THAT I AM. Tell them I AM sent you." (Exodus 3:13-14)

God can say I AM OMNISCIENT (all-knowing). He knows everything. As a matter of fact, He IS EVERY-THING. He certainly knows what he is doing even when we don't know what we're doing. The more we trust in him, the more we can rest in the confidence that we follow Him where ever He leads especially when it doesn't make sense.

Number three.

God can see the result.

Have you ever seen a scary movie? You see that the villain is up to no good. The main character is usually a woman who is in a dark creepy house or out in the woods all by herself. She's getting ready to walk right into trouble. Because, we as the audience can see what is ahead, we scream and yell to the victim, "Don't go in there! Watch out! Get out of there!" We know good and well that the actress cannot hear us. That's how it is with God.

"Through faith we understand that the worlds were framed by the word of God, so that things which are seen were not made of things which do appear. Hebrews 11:3

" I am Alpha and Omega, the beginning and the end, the first and the last." Revelations 22:13

God is watching us on life's silver screen. Despite the fact that God has no beginning or end, He knows that we as finite beings need some structure. He gives us the gift of time. He "frames" off blocks of time in our life just like the movie reel contains visible squares of division on the celluloid strip. He can see where we are headed before we can see it. Like the audience in the movie theater or before the T.V. screen, He can warn us of danger and order our steps. Unlike the actress on the screen, we can hear Him through the Holy Spirit, either gently whispering or outright shouting. We choose to heed or not to heed. The kind of result depends on us.

Number four.

God wants to demonstrate his awesome power.

There is a story told in the 9th chapter of John about a man that had been blind since his birth. (It's interesting that the story unfolds telling us that Jesus already knew the man had been blind since birth.) The disciples asked Jesus had this man or his parents had sinned. It was a commonly held notion that if a person suffered from certain maladies, it had to be the result of sin or wrongdoing in the person's life. Although some sickness is caused by our disobedience, other sicknesses are used by God to leave no doubt in any one's mind that the deliverance and the healing had to come through Jesus Christ.

"Jesus answered, Neither hath this man sinned, nor his parents: but that the works of God should be made manifest in him." John 9:3

For the lack of a better phrase, God is a "showoff." And rightly so. He is worthy of every bit of our praise. We sometimes tend to minimize the awesome power of God. We want others to think it happened because of our own works, so that we may be lifted up. He is a jealous God.

"Thou shalt not bow down thyself to them [idols] , nor serve them: for I the Lord thy God am a jealous God, visiting the iniquity of the fathers upon the children unto the third and fourth generation. of them that hate me." Exodus 20: 5

"......I will not give my glory to another." Isaiah 48:11

Sometimes, He moves in such a miraculous and supernatural way, that He makes it impossible for anyone to dispute his omnipotence (all - power). There will always be some skeptics. It had to be more skeptics then than now because they did not have the written record like we have. Little did they realize that denying the awesomeness of God would block further blessing that would be passed down through their generations.

When we obey God, even in those times that it just doesn't make sense, we are not the only ones that will be blessed. The family, the witnesses, and the observers will also have the opportunity to reap blessings. And sometimes it can start out from one seemingly insignificant act. If we recall the account of Peter's invitation to become a disciple, we will notice this very thing in Luke 5:1-11. We will also see how the levels of blessing increased at each additional call of obedience.

First, Jesus asked Peter to push the ship out a little a little distance from the shore. (vs. 3) Jesus wanted to tranform the ship into a stage in order for more people to see and hear his teachings. It seemed like such an insignificant act given the fact that it wasn't being used at the time. After all, they hadn't caught any fish anyway. They were going to wash their nets and call it a day.

At this first level, the people that heard him teach received the spiritual blessing through His word.

After Jesus had finished speaking to the crowd, He told Peter to launch out or go where the water was deep and cast the nets for a catch. (vs. 4). This request was stranger than the first. Peter, an expert fisherman, must have wondered how could someone just come up and instruct him about catching fish especially since they gone out earlier and had not caught nothing. Peter was not a new employee. Him and his brothers had done this all their lives. They knew when to fish, where to fish, how to fish, what bait to use, what lure would be best, you name it, they lived fish. They depended on this line of work for their survival. And Peter, being the outspoken man that he was, did not hesitate to bring Jesus up on the situation. *As if Jesus didn't know already.*

"Master, we have toiled all the night, and have taken nothing; nevertheless at thy word I will let down the net." (vs. 5)

I'm glad Peter said "nevertheless." In other words, Peter was saying, I know this doesn't make sense but it's worth giving it a try. Who knows what will happen? What do I have to lose?

Sometimes, it comes a point in our life, that we have tried everything. Nothing seems to work. Then the Counselor steps in and changes all that we thought we knew and gives us some advice that is contrary to our experiences. We can either rely on our narrow view or say like Peter, nevertheless. In doing this some more people were about to be blessed.

When Peter *and those with him,* did what Jesus said, they caught so many fish, that the nets broke from the weight of all that bounty. Peter and his crew had to call over the neighboring ships to help with this tremendous catch. (vs. 6-7) These first two submissions of obedience led to both spiritual and material blessings for a lot of folks. They had enough fish to open a seafood restaurant, hold a fish fry fellowship and feed the people who had just heard Jesus teaching!

But it didn't stop there. Peter was so taken by the experience, that he felt too unworthy to even stand before Jesus. Peter felt he did not even deserve to be in the presence of such awesomeness. Was Jesus going to strike him dead? After all, how could Peter withstand such power from the Holy One and still live? (vs.8 -9) *But God knew the plan for Peter.* Jesus announced that Peter was going to be responsible for a much higher calling. Peter was going to catch men's souls and point them to the One who could truly rescue them. O, just think about how many thousands of souls have been blessed and saved through the ministry of Peter even to this day!

What would have happened if these patriarchs and matriarchs decided to bend to popular opinion? Where would we be in this day and time if they thought God's commands were too silly to follow? Look at what we would have lacked.

God does not want us to be exclusive receivers but inclusive donors. God has invested His best in us. He expects us to earn interest on it. If you are a child of God, expect to be used by Him. We are his vessels to give glory to His name. Beware that we may not always feel comfortable and safe when asked to do the "ridiculous" thing for God. But remember, if it's backed up in His Word, He will always be with us. He will always reward those that obey him. *Even those that obey Him as innocent bystanders.*

We should want God to do for us the same thing that he did for Jesus. When we are humbly submitted to God, He will exalt us. Being a joint heir (Romans 8:17) makes Jesus our big brother.

"Let this mind be in you, which was also in Christ Jesus: Who being in the form of God though it not robbery to be equal with God. But made himself of no reputation and took upon him the form of a servant and was in the likeness of men. And being found in the fashion as a man, he humbled himself and became obedient unto death, even the death of the cross. Wherefore God hath highly exalted him, and given him a name which is above every name. That at the name of Jesus every knee shall bow.... And that every tongue should confess that Jesus Christ is Lord...." Philippians 2:5-11

Chapter 8

MENTALITY

My parents would never be considered millionaires by the world's definition. However, I do not recall a time that we went lacking for anything. And I do mean anything. Besides the fact, that there was always food, water and lights, there was also plenty of family love and support. After my father passed, my mother remained living in the house that I had been raised in. She paid $48.00 a month. ($60.00 when there was a fifth Sunday!) That was truly a blessing. We're talking about from the 1950's to the mid 90's. But later, the time came that Mama had to move, because the house was going to be torn down. Mama had lived in that house for over forty years. What would she do now? It would be no way she could find anything at the price she was paying. However, Mama was not worried. As a matter of fact, I was more worried than she was. We looked around and found a little two bedroom cottage that was just right for her. The rent was $380.00. Little did I know, that Mama was wise enough to know the importance of "saving for the rainy day." When the time to came to pay the deposit and first month's rent, she went into what she called her "bammer" and easily retrieved $640.00 without breaking a sweat! Mama knew that everything she would ever need, including wisdom and planning, came from the Lord. My desire is not to just look like a million bucks but BE a million bucks. It all starts with the way we think.

"I have been young and now am old; yet I have not seen the righteous forsaken nor his seed begging bread. He is ever merciful and lendeth and his seed IS blessed." Psalm 37:25-26.

Most Christians tend to take the scripture and give the false impression that everything should be 100% spiritually interpreted. And although the priority will always be that we know Him "in spirit and in truth," our Lord is concerned about the "whole" person. David even relates that as long as He could remember, that God was with the righteous. When we say that we are righteous, we are saying we are in "right standing" with God. The standard that we are measured by is His Word. It's not enough for Him to just be with us: he will not see his *seed* (us and the generations to follow) groveling on the ground for just a crumb of bread. He's not just talking about spiritual bread which is the word. He's also talking about food and finances. He never intended for his seed to be "level to the ground" or "just make it ." With him being ever merciful, this sheds light on the fact he continually wants to give to us. His lending is not Him wanting us to pay him back, like we would pay back a loan. He desires his seed to be blessed to in turn bless others in return. We have to be careful that we don't become so "heavenly bound" that we become no "earthly good."

Let's consider a biblical case in point. In the nineteenth chapter of Matthew, a story unfolds about a rich young ruler.

This young man wanted to know what could he do to obtain eternal life. Jesus started by running down the heavy weight commandments—no murdering, no hanky panky with other people's spouses, no stealing, no lying (white lies or any other color), obeying parents, and loving neighbors as you love yourself. Jesus set the priorities or the most important issues first which boiled down to being obedient in keeping the commandments. The young man had no problem with that. He had been there and done that. Jesus said, "Well, alright then. But if you want to be perfect…perfect?!!! The rich young man must have wondered at the term perfect. He just wanted to live a long time. Jesus goes on to say that if the young ruler wanted to be perfect, it would be necessary to sell what he had and give it to the poor. Jesus went on further to explain that in doing this, he would have treasure in heaven. Now, I call that a "high interest" return and a win—win situation. But the young man turned away and walked off sorrowfully. He was so blinded by his material possessions that he couldn't see the future interest.

This still happens. Whether we are speaking of financial investments such as stocks or bonds to yield returns for a comfortable retirement 20 years from now or if we are contemplating the decision of salvation, wondering if we're going to miss out on all the fun and glitz now for a promise of eternal life. Sin has perpetuated this mindset to produce generational poverty. But the curse can be broken. It's all in the mind.

"And be not conformed to this world; but be ye transformed by the renewing of your mind, that ye may prove what is that good, and acceptable and perfect, will of God." Romans 12:2

The states of your mind is like the changes that water can undergo. Water can be a liquid that takes the shape of whatever container it is in. That's like conforming to the world. You go along and fit into whatever mode the world is in at the time. But if water changes to a solid like ice or gas, it can no longer fit into anything. As ice, it would have a more *acceptable* use to cool down a drink or keep a bruise from swelling. As a gas, it would be *perfect* in an iron to smooth out wrinkles in clothes or signal that the water for that nice cup of tea is ready. God desires that our minds be renewed in every aspect of our lives. And as we study the word of God prayerfully, our minds will begin to grasp a more balanced picture of this thing we call abundant life. If we don't "rightly divide the word of truth." (II Timothy 2:15b), we will consistently live beneath our God -given privileges. It's a mind game.

Chapter 9

GETTING A FAIR
SLICE OF THE PIE

Rightly dividing the Word of God is like dividing a good 'ole sweet potato pie. If you don't cut up that pie equally, somebody is going to get mad. Somebody is going to get a small slither which isn't enough. Or somebody is going to get a big old hunk, which is going to seem unfair to the person that got the slither or that person will be considered as just straight out greedy. We must God to help us apply the scriptures to our everyday lives to clearly see what His real plan is for every episode in our lives. If we don't, we will feel slighted in some areas and overwhelmed in others. Let's rightly divide two biblical stories that usually sabotages Christians about money matters.

The first story found in Luke 12:16-22 tells the story of a rich man whose land yielded an abundance of harvest. We discover that this man was rich from the beginning. What is the significance of knowing that? We must realize that children of God are already rich in every sense of the word because we are already joint-heirs with Christ. (Romans 8:17) The defining factor is how we utilize our inheritance. Initially in this story, there was nothing wrong in considering what to do with this increase. (v. 17) It was even appropriate to make plans to make more room. After all, God would not want for use to allow the harvest to rot or go to waste. (v 18) The initial folly is the fact that the man magnifies himself so much that he thinks it is time to only think about himself. He has a false sense of security based on nothing but what his own efforts have produced. Secondly, there is no evidence that this brother was going to share his bounty with anyone.

God's pin of reality pops the bubble of self reliance and announces that this fool—yes, he said fool— would die that very night. Psalm 14:1 defines a fool as "one that has said in his heart there is no God." A fool is a person who completely lacks spiritual understanding or sensitivity. Without acknowledging God, we are all fools. Fools are sinners. Predictably, if we don't consider God, we are certainly not going to think about His children. God further drives home the point when he raises an eye-opening question. "Then whose (which of God's children or even your own children) shall have these things (which you are leaving behind) which thou hast provided (or hoarded)? Proverbs 13:22 provides us with the supportive fact that the "riches of the wicked (sinful ones) are laid up for the righteous (ones in right standing with God through the blood of Jesus) God concludes in this story by reminding us that this is true for everyone that lays up treasure for himself and is not rich toward God and his children. The wonderful flip side of this is that You can lay up material and spiritual treasure and invest in God and his children and still won't go broke!

Let us look at the second case study. This is similar to the first but with a twist.

"There was a certain rich man, which was clothed in purple and fine linen and fared sumptuously everyday: And there was a certain beggar named Lazarus, which was laid at his gate, full of sores. to be fed with the crumbs which fell from the rich man's table: moreover the dogs came and licked his sores. And it came to pass, that the beggar died, and was carried by the angels into Abraham's bosom: the rich man also died and was buried. And in hell he lift up his eyes, being in torments, and seeth Abraham afar off, and Lazarus in his bosom. Luke 16: 19-23.

Besides supplying supporting evidence that there is truly a hell, we can learn another deeper lesson about stewardship.

Let me make a confession. I don't want to just look or appear saved and in right standing with God. *I am saved and in right standing with God.* In the same respect, I don't just want to appear rich with all the outside trappings. I don't want clothes I can't afford. I don't want expensive cars I can't maintain. I desire to be rich in every sense of the word. This rich man was not an imposter. He was the real Bill Gates of his day. People know when you are for real because they tend to draw closer to you and want to know what and how you got what you got. It was obvious to Lazarus and maybe others that this man could offer some relief. Whether Lazarus was placed at the gate or came on his own, the rich man's reputation was known.

The rest of the story describes how both men died. Lazarus went to heaven and the rich man went to hell. Hell was so tormenting that the rich man desired that Lazarus would dip the tip of his finger in water and sooth his parched tongue. Why did they end up at different destinations? After all, poor people can go to hell and rich people can go to heaven. It is true that the rich man should have assisted Lazarus in life. (v. 25) Certainly, he had the means to do so. But the clincher is in verse 26.

"And beside all this, between us and you there is a great gulf fixed: so that they which pass from hence to you cannot; neither can they pass to us, that would come from hence.

This shows us that "beside all this" including the ignoring and lack of compassion for Lazarus, there was something more that kept them apart. The gulf was a result of unbelief in God. How do we know that? We know this by the message that the rich man wanted Abraham to relay to his living brothers through Lazarus.

"Then he (rich man) said, I pray thee therefore, father, that thou wouldest send him to my father's house: For I have five brethren that he may testify unto them lest they also come into this place of torment. Abraham saith unto him, they have Moses and the prophets; let them hear them. And he said, Nay, father Abraham: but if one went unto them from the dead, they will repent. And he said unto him, if they hear not Moses and the prophets, neither will they be persuaded, though one rose from the dead. (vs. 27-31)

What did the rich man want his brothers to be warned about? Warned to give more? Warned to not be rich? Certainly these would not be warnings of the prophets like Moses and others. Their message was always of pointing people to God through Jesus Christ through types and shadows throughout the Old Testament. He knew that his brothers needed to heed to the call of repentance. That is making a spiritual U-turn in their life and believing.

This request could not be granted, even if Lazarus wanted to. Abraham, in conclusion, pointed out that if the brothers did not heed to the live prophets of their day, what would persuade them if the message came as a result of a séance of the dead.

So our mind set should be to rightly divide God's truth.

It's more than just thinking about treasures and they miraculously fall in your lap. It is more about putting in proper perspective what God has already provided and putting it to use through proper application of His word. This will bring forth a fruitful and balanced harvest.

God has sowed seeds of the word. The question is if our heart's soil been broken up to accept it to yield a fruitful harvest. Jesus gives a description of this as he opens up to his disciples four heart soil conditions and the harvest results.

"...The seed is God's message. The seed that fell on the hard path represents those who hear the message, but then the Devil comes and steals away and prevents them from believing and being saved. The rocky soil represents those who hear the word with joy. But like young plants in such soil, their roots don't go very deep. They believe for a while, but they wilt when the hot winds of testing blow. The thorny ground represents those who hear and accept the message, but all too quickly the message is crowded out by the cares and riches and pleasures of this life. And so they never grow into maturity. But the good soil represents honest, good hearted people who hear God's message, cling to it, and steadily produce a huge harvest." Luke 8:11-15 (New Living Translation)

What is the condition of your heart soil? Even if your heart is in one of the first three conditions, God can break it up and fertilize it and make it useful. He wants you to bring forth an abundant harvest. Despite the conditions, in our society, God's plan for you is abundance in every sense of the Word.

"The thief cometh not, but for to steal, and to kill, and to destroy. I am come that they might have life, and that they might have it more abundantly." John 10:10

My God is not an Enron CEO. Think about it.

Chapter 10

Love + Gift = Increase

"A man's gift maketh room for him and
bringeth him before great men."
Proverbs 18:16

My mother was a natural entrepreneur. She had the talent of preparing food that was so good that it would make you want to slap somebody. She just didn't cook. She *loved* to cook. In contrast, I only cook so my children will not starve and that my husband will not divorce me (smile). She never saw cooking as drudgery. Hers was a labor of love.

If you mentioned that you were sick, she would fix you up a pot of soup or send you over a jar of pot liquor (that's the juice from cooking greens) and people would swear that it cured what ailed you. It didn't matter if she knew you for a long time or if you were a stranger. No one would starve under her watch.

She cooked and sold dinners for a multitude of fundraising efforts. She would cook some good old apple and sweet potato jacks and sandwiches to take to Daddy's job at lunchtime to sell. She even cooked and sold Yock (a Chinese dish) to help my high school purchase uniforms.

I remember fondly how Mama cooked complete dinners for a family during the holidays like Easter, Christmas and Thanksgiving. When the wife passed away, Mama continued to cook for the gentleman and his children—every week. He paid her well. Why was this significant? Well, the family was White and my mama was Black. No, it was not slavery time. She did this up until three months before her death in 1996. It didn't matter. There was a need and Mama practiced compassion.

She would call me many times and say, "Gayle, don't worry about fixing dinner tomorrow. Just stop by my house after work and pick it up after you get off from work." That was music to a busy mother and family.

We need to use our *gifts* that we have been given by the creator.

We need to pause a moment and make sure that we understand what a gift from God is. *A talent is not a gift.* A talent in the biblical sense is the manifestation or evidence of the God- given gift.

I have discovered in studying the gifts of the God-Head, each component of the trinity consists of gifts. Gifts of the Father are prophecy, ministry, teaching, exhortation, giving, leadership and mercy. (Romans 12:3-8) The gifts of the Son are apostles, prophets, evangelists, pastors, and teachers. (Ephesians 4:11)

The gifts of the Holy Spirit are the word of wisdom, the word of knowledge, faith, healing, working of miracles, prophecy, discerning of spirits, different kinds of tongues and the interpretation of tongues.

Therefore, my mother's talent for cooking was a manifestation of giving, and showing mercy from God. When she delivered the food, and shared the Word with it she was being an evangelist in which Christ was pleased with. The Holy Spirit led her to drop a word of wisdom and knowledge to someone that needed it before they broke the physical bread. I already told you that there was healing in the soup.

Love makes it all come together.

"Eagerly desire the greater gifts. But now, let me show you the most excellent way. If I could speak in any language in heaven or on earth but didn't love others, I would only be making meaningless noise like a loud gong or a clanging cymbal. If I had the gift of prophecy, and if I knew all the mysteries of the future and knew everything about everything, but didn't love others, what good would I be? And if I had the gift of faith so that I could speak to a mountain and make it move, without love I would be no good to anybody. if I gave everything I have to the poor and even sacrificed my body, I could boast about it; but if I didn't love others, I would be of no value whatsoever. Love is patient and kind. Love is not jealous or boastful or proud or rude. Love does not demand it own way. Love is not irritable, and keeps no record of when it has been wronged. It is never glad about injustice but rejoices whenever the truth wins out. Love never gives up, never loses faith, is always hopeful, and endures through every circumstance. Love will last forever, but prophecy and speaking in tongues and special knowledge will all disappear. For even our special knowledge is incomplete. But when the end comes, these special gifts will all disappear. It's like this: When I was a child, I spoke and though and reasoned as a child does. But when I grew up, I put away childish things. Now we see things imperfectly as in a poor mirror, but then we will see everything with perfect clarity. All that I know now is partial and incomplete, but then I will know everything completely, just as God know me

now. There are three things that will endure—faith, hope and love—and the greatest of these is love."
(I Corinthians 12:31 - 13:1-13 New Living Translation)

We must not confuse singing in the church choir, ushering on the board, or serving in religious organizations as gifts. We must *exercise or use* the God -given gift in the singing, ushering and serving. To give an example of this, we know that there are many talented gospel singers. No matter how beautiful the singer sings, if there is no exhortation (lifting up Jesus) or teaching, it has no effect. We can tell when singers are just moving their lips and nothing else. An usher is not exercising her gifts if she or he doesn't smile or show mercy when greeting and seating people. Auxiliaries are not operating in their gifts if there is no sharing, giving or spiritual leadership. We need to use our gifts that has been given by the Creator. And when we mingle these gifts with sincere concerns for others, it will put us in positions where men will supply what we need.

And yes, every child of God has gifts. Pray that the Lord would show you yours, especially if it has been lying dormant.

"Neglect not the gift that is in you, which was given thee by prophecy with the laying on of the hands of the presbytery." I Timothy 4:14

"...Stir up the gift of God, which is in thee by the putting on of my hands." II Timothy 1:6

God has laid his nail-scarred hands on you. Power are in those hands to strengthen you to utilize those gifts that will not only bless His people but will also set you up for a fruitful life.

We still can't get away from the importance of obedience

even when pondering how to use our gifts and talents. Consider the story of the talents.

"Again, the Kingdom of Heaven can be illustrated by the story of a man going on a trip. He called together his servants and gave them money to invest for him while he was gone. He gave five bags of gold to one, two bags of gold to another and one bag of gold to the last—dividing it in proportion to their abilities—and then left on his trip.. The servant who received five bags of gold began immediately to invest the money and soon doubled it. The servant with two bags of gold also went right to work and doubled the money. But the servant to who received the one bag of gold dug a hole in the ground and hid the master's money for safekeeping. After a long time their master returned from his trip and called them to give an account of how they had used his money. The servant to whom he had entrusted the five bags of gold said, 'Sir, you gave me five bags of gold to invest, and I have doubled the amount.' The master was full of praise. 'Well done, my good and faithful servant. You have been faithful in handling this small amount, so now I will give you many more responsibilities. Let's celebrate together!' Next came the servant who had received the two bags of gold, with the report, 'Sir, you gave me two bags of gold to invest and I have doubled the amount.' The master said , 'Well done, my good and faithful servant. You have been faithful in handling this small amount, so now I will give you many more responsibilities. Let us celebrate together!' Then the servant with the one bag of gold came and said, Sir, I know you are a hard man, harvesting crops you didn't plant and gathering crops you didn't cultivate. I was afraid I would lose your money, so I hid it in the earth and here it is. But the master said, ' You wicked and lazy servant! you think I'm a hard man, do you, harvesting crops I didn't plant and gathering crops I didn't cultivate? Well you

should have least have put my money into the bank so I could have some interest. Take the money from this servant and give it to the one with the ten bags of gold. To those who use well what they are given, even more will be given, and they will have an abundance. But from those who are unfaithful, even what little they have will be taken away. Now throw this useless servant into outer darkness, where there will be weeping and gnashing of teeth.'"

Matthew 25:14-30 (New Living Translation)

We wonder why God blesses some people more than others. God knows who He can invest in. God expects an increase for what He plants in us.

As this story unfolds, we discover that the master of these servants is going away on a trip and he leaves money to them. The purpose was to do something with it to increase its value. He gives amounts according to who He already knew would do the most with it. You might ask, "Well, if He already knew what the fella was going to do with the money, why give him any in the first place?" I'm glad God is not man. Since He's a merciful God, he still is trying to draw us and sometimes He wants to see what we're going to do if given the chance.

"Not slothful in business, fervent in spirit; serving the Lord" Romans 12:11

The enemy has a way of working through slothfulness and procrastination that allows him time to plant seeds of distrust and faithlessness. That's why the servant with the one bag hid his. As we see in his explanation, one of his problems was that he spent his time trying to analyze his master. He had too much time on his hands. He was talking about how hard the master was and what the master did and did not do. That was not any of his concern!

On the other hand the other two, worked and accepted the responsibility and doubled their master's money. They took little and made much.

If you cannot handle the small stuff, why do you think God is going to trust you with big stuff? If you can't take your meager paycheck and give God his tithe and pay your bills with the other ninety percent, why would He give you a million dollars to waste even more?

"....For unto whomsoever much is given, of him shall be much required..." Luke 12:48

If you cannot rule and control your own house, why would God entrust you with a mega-church? How do you plan to feed thousands, when you turned your next door neighbor away that needed a slice of bread? How can we say we love God, and don't speak to the person sitting in the pew next to us in church?

When we love our Master, the Heavenly Father, by utilizing the gifts He has given us, we illuminate His glory. And when we do that, his glory will be so great that it will be no way that it will miss us in all aspects.

Chapter 11

BLESSED TO BE
A BLESSING

S ometimes I think about the time that Jesus fed the five thousand with the two fish and five loaves of bread. It happened to be a little boy's lunch. I know Jesus would have fed those folks in a supernatural way regardless if the boy was there or not. But what if the boy's mother had no concern even for her own son and just sent him out there with no food? (By the way, that seems like a whole lot of food for a boy, especially five loaves of bread!) The mother created an opportunity for her little boy to be a blessing without even knowing it.

"If a brother or sister be naked and destitute of daily food and one of you say unto them, Depart in peace, be ye warmed and filled; notwithstanding ye give them not those things

which are needful to the body, what doth it profit? Even so faith, if it hath not works, is dead, being alone. James 2:15-17

A lot of you are saying right now, "All I *can* do is pray for the brother or sister' cause I don't have anything to give!" That's why I believe so strongly in Christians being prosperous even in their material finances and resources.

From a soul-winning aspect, it is a poor commentary for us to claim we are King's Kids. Who would want to serve a destitute God that doesn't even take care of his own?

We love to rehearse the story about the lame man that was sitting at the gate called Beautiful, begging alms in Acts 3. You know the story when Peter and John passed by and they told the lame man, "Look on us." Peter and John said they had no money, but what they had *was what he needed at this particular time.* If you notice the 5th verse, it only said he *expected* to receive something from them. That something was money. After all, that's what he was there for day after day. He did not *need* the money. Peter and John realized that his need was healing. *Money had not taken care of his need.* It did not help him to walk in the past. When a person is hungry, he *needs* food, not healing. When a person is naked, he *needs* clothes, not food. Offering salvation to a person who has not eaten for days will not work. The volume of his growling stomach will be louder than anything you may say. A child that has no coat to shield him from the elements of winter cannot concentrate on the prayer you are praying, because the concept of survival has taken precedence. We cannot offer people substitutes as bandages. We have to get to the bottom of their true *need.* The Christian that is prosperous in Spirit, Word *and* resources is the most effective.

It baffles me to think that with all the churches in our nation, that there are still thousands of people that are destitute in spirit and resources. There are churches on every corner. There are even two and three churches that stand side by side on the same street block. If churches were really about their purpose, there would be no need for government to bear the majority of the welfare burden. The church should not only be a place of spiritual refuge but also an institution that takes care of peoples' needs and provides the means for people to learn to take care of themselves. The early church is a model that we should consider.

"And all that believed were together, and had all things common; And sold their possessions and goods, and parted them to all men, as every man had need. And, they, continuing daily with one accord in the temple, and braking bread from house to house, did eat their meat with gladness and singleness of heart. Praising God, and having favour with all the people. And the Lord added to the church daily such as should be saved." Acts 2:44-47

First, they believed.
Believed in what?
They believed in the Lord and Savior Jesus Christ.
They were saved.
They were born again.
They were converted.
They were new creatures.

"...If thou wilt confess with thou mouth the Lord Jesus and believe in thine heart that God hath raised him from the dead, thou shalt be saved. For with the heart man believeth unto righteousness; and with the mouth confession is made unto salvation." Romans 10:9-10

This is always priority.
This should always be the prerequisite.

Then they shared what they had. Some had businesses and

occupations through which they could be blessings to others. They were not stingy. They shared everything among themselves *first*.

The unity, love and togetherness was so contagious that it drew sinners to be saved daily.

Imagine what would happen if churches were like that today. I believe that the walls of brick and mortar have made churches to be more like exclusive clubs rather than the called out body of believers. It must be understood that early churches were bodies of people that moved about sharing the gospel. The temple was the common place to for worship, praising and learning God's word. The temple was never meant to be a religious day club.

We, especially, as Christians must make ourselves a committee of one to seek opportunities to be blessings to others. We do that by having faith in God that He will first supply our needs and add to us. In turn, we can plant seeds in others, spiritually and materially, so they can in turn become blessings to others.

I like to call it revolving credit with outstanding interest.

Chapter 12

JESUS BLESS AMERICA

Have you ever took the time to wonder why you were born in America? You could have been born anywhere in the world. Your parents could have been African, Caucasian, European, Indian, Pakistani, Eskimo, Hispanic, etc. They could have been anything opposite of what you are right now. You could have been born in a disease ridden or famine starved third world country. Yes, I am proud to be an American.

Why? I'm glad you asked another good question! You may say that America is not perfect. It's not. You may say that there is so much crime and violence. We do. Prejudice and indifference resides here. Yes, that's right. But despite all of that, there's one thing that makes America stand head and shoulders above the rest. The fact is that this nation was rooted and grounded on a foundation based on the Word of God. That is what truly makes us a free country.

"And ye shall know the truth, and the truth shall make

you free." John 8:32

And though many nations profess to recognize that there is a God, they fall short when they fail to recognize that Jesus, the Son, is the way to God the Father. You will never see the phrase, Jesus Bless America, One Nation under Jesus, and In Jesus We Trust. Why? It is easier to use God as a generic or a catch-all, than to give honor to the One that is truly worthy; the One that bridges us to the Father and Holy Spirit.

"..I am the way, the truth, and the life: no man cometh unto the Father, but by me." John 14:6

What a wonderful truth! Although we may be restrained by the invisible chains of sin and even the physical bars of incarceration, we have the opportunity to be free in every aspect of our life through Christ.

And what are we free from? We are free from the devil's control of our minds and actions. This gives us choices to serve God. When we serve and obey God, the world is ours to utilize to His glory.

Notice God's order for "his people."

"If my people, which are called by my name, shall humble themselves, and pray and seek my face, and turn from their wicked ways; THEN will I hear from heaven and will I hear from heaven and will forgive their sin and will heal their land." II Chronicles 7:14

Humans are not born as adults and grow into babies. Students do not receive high school diplomas and then go to 12 years of school. People are not given driving licenses first and then learn how to drive. That's not the order. God has supernatural plans for us as a nation but we must make the choice to do it His way and in order.

A lot of times we want to take the above verse backwards. Lord, heal my land. (The "land" that needs to be healed may be our souls. It may be our physical bodies. It may be our financial situations. It may be the landscape of our relationships.) Lord, forgive us. Hear me Lord.

See we're backwards.

But it must start with relationship. In the beginning of my life, my parents prayed and trained me to walk in the paths of righteousness. But I had to make the choice to have a personal relationship with Jesus Christ for myself. I had to be one of his people. Besides the physical birth, I had to be born again so that I could be in God's family. . "For God so loved the world (I'm so glad that you and I are included) that he gave (free gift) his only begotten Son, that whosoever (that's anybody) believeth (just trust him by faith) on him shall not perish (live) but have everlasting life. (on earth and in heaven too.!) Now, I have a name that he can call me by.

Because He is in control of our lives, we humble ourselves or make ourselves low unto him. We don't dictate to him because he has us in his best interest and we can't see what is ahead. Only He knows that.

We've got to communicate with him through prayer because that strengthens our relationship with him. I'm not talking about begging him for something all the time. Let me use this example. My husband and I have been married a little over twenty years. Just imagine how it would be if I only talked to him on Sundays, once a week or on a very inconsistent basis. Or worse yet, when I did talk to him, I only asked him to buy me something. He wants me to talk with him daily. He wants me to know what is on his mind and he wants to know what is on my mind. He wants to know that I still love him and that he is fine. He wants me to thank him for being a good husband, father and friend. God is no different. As a matter of fact, He is jealous (Exodus 20:5) when we don't give our all to him. "I will not give my glory to another"

(Isaiah 48:11)

Next, we've got to seek his face. He wants us to look for him. God wants us to study his word, to know his mind. The more we seek him and discover more of who He is, we can be more like him. There is an old song of the church that the saints used to sing:

> *To be like Jesus, to be like Jesus,*
> *Oh how I long (long was stretched out*
> *...Loooooonnnggg)*
> *To be like him.*
> *So meek and lowly, so humble and holy.*
> *Oh how I long to be like him.*

Every time I heard that song, it made me think that it would be a struggle or a impossibility to be like Jesus, especially the way they sung it. That's what the enemy wants you to think, too. That's why you have to make the conscious choice to turn from your wicked ways.

You say that you can't stop sinning. You are absolutely right. YOU, by yourself, cannot do it. It is only through the power of God. You may ask, "Do you mean that I can be perfect? That I will not make any mistakes? Do you mean I'm going to dot every "i," and cross every "t?" Well, if you think I'm going to say, "Well, really, you know you can't do that because after all, we're only **human."** Wrong. Sorry. I am going to say that we can be righteous because you can be in "right standing" with God. How, you say? By making sure that how we live and how we conduct our lives line up with God's standards which are outlined in His word. Remember, we're measured by God's yardstick not man's.

God does not wish for us to be robots. He gives us choice but he does pull the strings as a divine puppet master. He guides us on the stage of life and presents us to God and the world not as merely struggling artists but Oscar-winning stars!

Chapter 13

SEASONS

I t is said that every phase of our life represents a season. Just as seasons change from new-beginning springs to breath-taking summers transitioning into golden autumns and brisk winters, our lives go through similar episodes.

Sometimes it appears that our seasons are not proportioned. That is, for example, we may stay in a deep freeze for a long period before that thaw finally comes. We ask many times, when will my breakthrough come through.

This is certainly true when it comes to a point in our lives that we ask when our proverbial "ship will come in." And we are usually referring to those financial ships. Sometimes when we read Galatians 6:9, we want to say .... yeah, right.

"And let us not be weary in well doing: for in due season we shall reap, if we faint not.

We get frustrated and we ask, "but when will our due season ever come? I've been stuck in winter for so long." One thing we can be sure of is that God does not lie and his word will not come void.

I've got to go back to some music. Donald Lawrence and the Tri-City Singers have two hits on their CD "Go Get Your Life Back" that describes this so well. The first track is "The Best is Yet to Come." It starts:

Hold on my brother, don't give up. Hold on my sister, just look up. There is a master plan in store for you, If you just make it through. God's gonna really blow your mind; He's gonna make it worth your while. After all the trouble you been through the blessing's doubled just for you.
The best is yet to come!

That's a really upbeat and uplifting message. But they come on the very next cut and sing the song "Seasons." One particular verse touches me especially:

I know you've invested a lot and the return has been slow, You throw up your hands and say I give up, just can't take this anymore. But I hear the Spirit say, it's your time, your wait is over; Walk into your season.

If you are a child in God's destiny, you have felt like this. Just be assured that it is a sure sign that you are about to walk into what God has for you.

This "walk" however is not just a stroll or glide into happiness. It's a consistent jog or press to the finish line.

"No, dear brothers and sisters, I am still not all I should be, but I am focusing all my energies on this one thing: Forgetting the past and looking forward to what lies ahead, I strain to reach the end of the race and receive the prize for which God, through Christ Jesus, is calling us up to heaven." Philippians 3:13-14.(NLT)

My season is in the up position. Everything is up. Eyes are up. Faith is up. Goals are up. Even if all the marathon runners are ahead of us, we have to keep on moving until we step smack dab in it. And still keep walking.

Consider David. When David was anointed a king, he did not immediately take over a kingdom as a king. As a matter of fact, the king at that time, Saul, was jealous of David. God had taken His favor from Saul. The women singing the praises of David over Saul also did not help matters either. Imagine the frustration of David being in the place but not in the place even after giant slaying, javelin dodging, and dealing with lions and bears. Oh my! There were even opportunities to kill Saul, but he maintained his integrity by declaring, "I will not touch God's anointed nor do His servant harm." But David's time did come. His patience and faithfulness awarded him the title of "a man after God's own heart." His lineage is always associated with the genealogy of Jesus Christ.

Yes, many of us have been in the same predicament. But our time is coming if we wait in expectation and service.

"Occupy until I come" Luke 19:13

Sometimes we think waiting means to sit twiddling our thumbs until something falls into our laps. If we look at what a waiter does in a restaurant, we know that he or she are actually serving. The customer places the order and the waiter fulfills the order. We are not occupying time and space in idleness. Let us be encouraged as we anticipate God's destined end. I can't say it any better that the conclusion of Donald Lawrence's song:

We're in a time when I believe God's gonna really
bless the saints,
Those who have stayed,

those who have prayed,
He's gonna fulfill the promise He made,
For I hear the spirit say,
It's your time, your wait is over.
Walk into your season.
You survived the worst of times,
God was always on your side,
State your claim, write your name,
Walk into the wealthy place.
The wait is over, it's your time.

Chapter 14

THE SAFE DEPOSIT BOX

My prayer is that God will bless everyone to come to the place that God would have them to come into. Sometimes, when God does come through, we may tend to forget how we got to that point. It would not be the first time in history that this has happen. Just like we suddenly get spiritual amnesia after God has delivered us from sickness, peril, and destitution, the children of Israel suffered the same malady.

"I spake unto thee in thy prosperity; but thou saidst, I will not hear. This hath been thy manner from thy youth, that thou obeyst not my voice. Jeremiah 22:21

Most of the time, when God does bless us, we forget who provided the means for us to become prosperous. We may start to slide to the I-did-it state of self righteousness. That's why we must go a step further and ask for God's keeping power. I believe we must maintain a spiritual safe deposit box of the word in us.

It's like my mama's chow-chow.

When I was growing up, my mama did a lot of preserving and canning. She was from the old school. She believed in preparing in the summer for those cold winters. She called it "preparing for war in the time of peace." She would gather and buy vegetables from the farmer down the street that had a big garden on his property. There were tomatoes, string beans and butterbeans to cook and steam. There were apples to core and pears to slice. Peppers and onions to slice and dice. She would start collecting and buying the Mason jars. She would wash the ones that were emptied from the last winter, discard the cracked and unusable and buy some more. These jars were unique because they had a cap and a seal.

Her specialty was a garnish that was called "chow chow" that you ate on top of a good old helping of collard greens or cabbage. It was made of green tomatoes, green peppers and onions. First she would set those cut-up vegetables down in a big white wash tin with some sprinkled alum and sugar. Then she would prepare a little cloth bag with pickling spice and tied the top with a piece of string and set it in that mixture overnight. By morning, all that seasoning would penetrate through and then she cooked it. That "sweet smelling savour" just lit up the whole house. Then she would fill those Mason jars all the way to the top with all those different delicacies. I could already imagine some pear preserves on a hot biscuit on a cold January day. She placed the lid on each opening of the jar and then screwed on the cap real tight. As a matter of fact, when I was helping her as I got older, she would say, "Gayle, make sure you tighten that cap so no air can get in or the stuff will spoil." Although our hands would be sore from tightening those caps, the process was not complete. As those jars cooled, you could hear each jar sound a loud "pop." That meant that a vacuum had formed and you would almost need a vice or a 200 pound man to open those jars again. But one thing was for sure, we would have food for a many season. Even at her death she had saved some jars of chow chow in the shed outside that she had prepared about four years before. We didn't know it was out there at first, but when we discovered it, I always believed that she had left this special gift for my son James because he loved it the most.

Like that chow chow in those Mason jars, God fills you with his Word which acts as a preservative . He can keep you like no one else can keep you. He can take the pieces of your life, even before you knew you had a life, and seal you so that no devil or anything can "pluck you out of his hand." He seals you so the prince of the air cannot contaminate you with his garbage and germs. Oh yes, it's possible to live a clean and holy life. And when the Lord gets ready to present you or "pour you out," you become a sweet garnish for his service. Even when we are rich.

We can still be sweet garnishes if we maintain our safe deposit box, where the rich word of God can be stored for safekeeping. Just like safe deposit boxes that we purchase or rent at banks, the sole purpose is to guard against theft or natural destruction. When we keep the word safe in our hearts, we keep Satan from stealing and bringing to destruction what God has planted from the beginning. There may be a day when we will not have the Bible in it's written form. Some third world countries are even experiencing this right now. David recognized the importance of keeping the word and the keeping power of the word.

"Thy word have I hid in my heart, that I might not against thee." Psalm 119:11

Jabez also acknowledged the importance of being kept

after coming into the place. He even prayed for it in advance.

"And Jabez called on the God of Israel, saying, Oh that thou wouldest bless me indeed, and enlarge my coast, and THAT THINE HAND MIGHT BE WITH ME, AND THAT THOU WOULDEST KEEP ME FROM EVIL, THAT IT MAY NOT GRIEVE ME! And God granted him that which he requested.

I want to provide you with some word that will keep you when you come into that awesome place that God has planned for you. On the next pages, I have provided some pertinent scriptures that you can meditate on as you seek to remain grounded in the event of your coming out. There is also some space for you to jot down some thoughts on these scriptures to refer back to keep you grounded when God brings you into that place of abundance he has for you.

This can also be a written legacy that you could share and leave for future generations as well. We as Christians should invest in the generations that will come behind us. Not only should we leave wills, stocks, bonds and material provisons but we should also leave a written record of the experiences about how God lead and directed our lives.

"A good man leaveth an inheritance to his children's children...." Proverbs 13:22

"Ye must be born again." John 3:7

First thing's first. Have you taken this first step? When? How?_____

_____

_____

_____

_____

_____

_____

_____

_____

_____

_____

_____

_____

_____

_____

_____

_____

*"...If thou shalt confess with thy mouth the Lord Jesus,
<u>and</u> shalt believe in thine heart that God
hath raised him from the dead, thou shalt be saved."
Romans 10:9*

Because of emotion, many people may go to the front of the church and confess with their mouth. When the pastor asks a person in front of a whole congregation if they believe on Jesus, they would be too embarrassed say "not quite." That's why we must believe deep down in our hearts. To be an effective Christian, one cannot happen without the other.

"Trust in the Lord with <u>all</u> thine heart and lean
not unto thine own understanding. In <u>all</u> thy ways,
acknowledge him and he shall direct thy paths.
Proverbs 3:5

The important word here is <u>all.</u> Sometimes we want to only trust God for the catastrophic events in our lives. I've got to depend on him for even breath!

What do you trust in the Lord for?

_____

_____

_____

_____

_____

_____

_____

_____

_____

"The steps of a good man are ordered
by the Lord and he delighteth in his way."
Psalm 37:23

God has to order or "line up" my walk with Him. God delights in every detail of my life.

What is the evidence of your walk with the Lord?

_____

_____

_____

_____

_____

_____

_____

"O taste and see that the Lord is good.
Blessed is the man that trusteth in him."
Psalm 34:8

This verse reminds me of when my children were young. I would try to broaden their tastes in food by giving them a little pinch of something. They would not know if they liked it unless they tasted it. When you experience just a taste of God's goodness, you want more and more. That man that puts all his trust in Him is happy and full of joy.

Have you had a taste of Jesus?

_____
_____
_____
_____
_____
_____
_____

"Standfast therefore in the liberty wherewith
Christ hath made us free, and be not entangled
again with the yoke of bondage."
Galatians 5:1

Christ has set us free from the bondage and chains of sin. We need to stay free. Let's not go back to slavery.

How are you free in Christ?

_____
_____
_____
_____
_____
_____
_____

*"This I say then, Walk in the Spirit,
and ye shall not fulfill the lust of the flesh."*
Galatians 5:16.

Be directed by the Holy spirit, not self. If you are directed by the spirit, you will not give in to the cravings of your flesh.

What are some ways that I can walk in the Spirit daily?

_____

_____

_____

_____

_____

_____

_____

_____

*"And be not drunk with wine,
wherein is excess; but be filled with the Spirit."*
Ephesians 5:18

Alcoholics and drunkards beware! Strong drink can dull and play tricks with your senses. Allow the Holy Spirit to fill and control you.

How have you let the Holy Spirit fill and control you?

_____

_____

_____

_____

_____

_____

_____

_____

"Put on the whole armour of God, that ye
may be able to stand against the wiles of the devil."
Ephesians 6:11

Soldiers do not fight battles without protection. How do
you think you can fight Satan without the protection of God?
Read verses 13 -18 for the specific pieces of equipment that
you will need. Make sure you have it all on and secure.

_____

_____

_____

_____

_____

_____

_____

_____

"Man shall not live by bread alone, but by
every word that proceedeth out the mouth of God."
Matthew 4:4

We need more than bread to sustain life. We must feed on
every word of God. As a matter of fact, God's bread will
also keep us supplied with Sunbeam, Wonder and Mary Jane
as well.

Are you on a "balanced" diet of the word? Share with
those that may need some help and encouragement.

_____

_____

_____

_____

_____

_____

_____

_____

"Study to show thyelf approved unto God,
a workman that needeth not to be ashamed,
rightly dividing the word of truth.
II Timothy 2:15

"Study" here means more than memorizing text and words for a test on Friday and not thinking about it again like we did in school. We must "work" the Word to be an employee that knows his stuff and can share it correctly.

"Pray without ceasing." I Thessalonians 5:17

My husband would probably divorce me if I only communicated with him once a week. The relationship would break down. I talk to my husband everyday and sometimes into the night. And when I talk to him, I'm not always begging him for something. I compliment him and thank him for all types of things— especially his kindness. Same with God.

How often do you have a conversation with God? This includes talking and listening.

_____
_____
_____
_____
_____
_____
_____
_____
_____
_____
_____
_____
_____

"Let everything that hath breath praise the Lord."
Psalm 150:6

David, the writer of the majority of the book of Psalms, loved to praise the Lord. Praise is what we do to acknowledge what God has done for us. Worship is recognizing who He is. This verse doesn't say just "every saved person" praise the Lord. If you don't know the Lord as your Savior, and you are reading this, you have breath. You are benefiting from the same air, earth, and all of creation that God hath made. He's worthy of <u>all</u> of our praise.

(However, if you are saved, you have even more to praise Him for!)

Write your own "psalm" of praise.

_____

_____

_____

_____

_____

_____

_____

_____

_____

_____

_____

_____

_____

_____

_____

_____

_____

_____

_____

_____

_____

_____

_____

"There hath no temptation taken you
but such as is common to man: but God is faithful,
who will not suffer you to be tempted above
that ye are able; but will with the temptation also make
a way to escape, that ye may be able to bear it."
I Corinthians 10:13

The sin is not the temptation itself. The yielding to it is. Even Jesus was tempted. God knows how much we can take. He doesn't necessarily remove the temptation. He provides an escape, usually his Word, if we choose to take it.

Name temptations that God has helped you resist.

_____

_____

_____

_____

_____

"If any of you lack wisdom, let him ask of God,
that giveth to all men liberally, and upbraideth not;
and it shall be given him."
James 1:5

There's no excuse for anyone to be ignorant. Just ask Him for wisdom. He is not stingy with it and will not ask it back once He gives it to you.

What would like to have more wisdom about?

_____

_____

_____

_____

_____

_____

"But be ye doers of the word and not hearers only,
deceiving your own selves."
James 1:22

Hearing the word is a start. We must act on it. Apply it to our daily lives. We're not fooling anyone, including God. The only one who is deceived is ourselves.

What are some scriptures that I need to apply to my daily life? _____

_____

_____

_____

_____

_____

"..If ye have faith as a grain of mustard seed, ye shall say
unto this mountain, remove hence to yonder place, it shall
remove and nothing shall be impossible unto you."
Matthew 17:20

A little faith goes a long way. Nothing is impossible with faith, not even mountain moving.

Lord, increase my faith!

"Submit yourselves therefore to God.
resist the devil, and he will flee from you."
James 4:7

Usually when this scripture is quoted, the "submit" part is left. It's like you can resist the devil on your own and it's like he's scared of you. You have got to have some reinforcement and that only comes from humbling ourselves. God gives us favor when we humble ourselves.

*"As newborn babes, desire the sincere milk of the word,
that ye may grow thereby."*
I Peter 2:2

New converts need to have a hunger for the word of God.
You can start with milk. Steak will choke you. If you don't
have that hunger, ask God for a hunger. A lot of times, new
converts lose that initial zeal and excitement because they
have no more fuel. The word supplies energy.

If you have recently been saved, and you lack a hunger
and thirst for the word, pray earnestly for that desire.

*"If we confess our sins, he is faithful and just to forgive us
our sins, and to cleanse us from all unrighteousness."*
I John 1:9

There is no sin, except for blasphemy of the Holy Spirit
which is not accepting the Lord as Christ, that will not be
forgiven. Thieves on the cross, suicide killers, The Jeff
Dahmers, the Sons of Sam, The Andrea Yates, The Susan
Smiths, The Darryl Strawberrys, The Allen Iversons, The
catholic priests etc. of this world can be forgiven when they
have a relationship with my BIG DADDY.

Is there something that you need to ask forgiveness for?
He's waiting!

*"Beloved, believe not every spirit, but try the spirits
whether they are of God: because many false prophets are
gone out into the world." I John 4:1*

Don't believe everything you hear or read, even this
book, unless you try it or put it up beside the word and
standards of God. The devil has many deceivers, even

those in sheep's' clothes.

What are you listening to?

"Not forsaking the assembling of ourselves together."
Hebrews 10:25

You need to be with people that have the same thing in common. That's why coming to church, to assemble together is important. We draw strength from our Christian brothers and sisters and it lets us know we are not alone.

If you do not have a church home, seek a Bible-studying church.

"Have faith in God." Mark 11:22

It's funny how we can believe that we will be paid on our jobs every two weeks or whatever when man tells us so, although he hasn't shown us any money up front. But we lack the faith in a God that owns everything. We question and doubt the all knowing and all powerful one. What's up with that?

Think about it.

Chapter 15

YES, YOU CAN
HAVE IT ALL

Yes, if you want to call me a prosperity teacher, I gladly accept to stand guilty as charged. We are King's kids. Our Daddy owns everything. We've just got to obey our Daddy and there is no limit to what Daddy will give us.

"The earth is the Lord's and everything in it. The world and all its people belong to him...Who may climb the mountain of the Lord? Who may stand in his holy place? Only those whose hands and hearts are pure, who do not worship idols and never tell lies. They will receive the Lord's blessing and have right standing with God their savior." Psalm 24:1,3-5 New Living Translation

I am not, however, a greed monger. Greed mongers give a one sided message. The emphasis is entirely on money and material gain. True prosperity teachers and preachers serve balanced meals. I must not only expect you to do all the giving but I must give back to you in return. We must not treat the Word of God as a buffet special, where we pick and choose what we will eat. We must have nourishment from each spiritual food group to develop at a normal rate. Christian Prosperity Advocates (CPA's) place salvation as the prime food group. Then practical help for everyday living completes the rest of the menu. Jesus was a master of this and other writers were inspired as well.

Seek ye first the kingdom of God and His righteousness

[Spiritual]
+
And all these things will be added unto you. Matthew 6:23
[Practical]

Beloved, I wish above all things that thou prosper and be in good health,
[Practical]
+
even as thy soul prospereth. III John 2

[Spiritual]

****

I came that they might have life,
[Spiritual]
+
and that they might have it more abundantly. John 10:10
[Practical]

It was mentioned earlier in the commercial break (Chapter 4), that God has led my husband and I. God has already been birthing supernatural creative strategies to bring this vision to pass. The thing that is going to be so different about this venture is that we will be blessing people. The purchase cost of this book will represent the first seed that people will be planting. The second seed, which is the most important, is the heart seed that will be planted if one just dares to read the Word in this book. This book is crammed with so much Scripture, people will be receiving a double portion of food, both spiritual and physical. Who ever heard of authors that write about being blessings actually sharing blessings—spiritually and financially? Well, you may ask, where will the money come from? It will come from us giving from the harvest of our previous sowing. The scripture declares the result.

"Give and it shall be given unto you; good measure, pressed down, shaken together, and running over, shall men give into your bosom. For with the same measure that ye mete withal it shall be measured to you again." Luke 6:38

You haven't seen nothing yet!

"Now unto him that is able to do exceedingly abundantly above all that we ask or think, according to the power that worketh in us, Unto him be glory in the church by Christ Jesus throughout all ages, world without end. Amen"
Ephesians 3:20-21

THANK YOU!

Your purchase of this book is a seed of investment to bless this ministry. It is also an act of sowing seed into your life for an abundant harvest!

I would love to come to your town to sign books, conduct workshops, or speak at your church or in your community. At each event, my husband and I will be also planting seeds by blessing some people with a tangible financial blessing. Many authors have written similar books but I feel we must not only "talk the talk" but "walk the walk" by being a live example and vessels of blessing to all of God's children.

E-mail me at
ggilmore29@hotmail.com
for more information.
(Please type "Seeds" for the subject)

Printed in the United States
821400001B

9 781591 604723